THE LEGEND OF ZAGABOO

Zagabook 1

This book is dedicated to my wife Becky, my
daughter Maddie, and my son Charlie (my little
guy). Whenever you need me, just tug your ear.

Love, Dad.

Visit Zagaboo.com for more books and Zagaboo trinkets!

A long time ago there lived a young farm boy named Jack. Jack wanted to help his mommy and daddy take care of the horses, chickens, pigs, and cows. However, Jack was scared of the animals and often hid in the big red barn behind the house where he could be alone and do what he loved best: carve wooden toys.

One late afternoon, Mommy and Daddy were worried they wouldn't get all the farm work done before sundown. Although they knew Jack was afraid of the animals, they asked if he could help milk a few cows.

Jack wanted to help so badly, but the cows seemed so big and scary. Jack knew he could milk cows. He had seen his parents do it hundreds of times, but he was too afraid to try. Jack started to cry. He turned and ran for the big red barn. Mommy started to follow him, but Daddy stopped her.

"He'll be fine sweetheart," Daddy said. "He just needs a little time alone. However, I hope he learns how to overcome his fears soon. We're going to need his help more and more around the farm."

Jack in the meantime had gone to his work area, picked up his chisel from his tool box, and began carving a chunk of walnut wood. Tears streamed down his face and plopped onto the wooden carving. As Jack whittled away, he wondered why he was scared of the animals. He didn't want to be afraid.

Jack was an excellent woodworker and carving always made him feel better. Because he was very upset that day, Jack worked extra hard to make his toy perfect. After a while, the lump of wood began to resemble a person, but it had long pointy ears, a big round nose, and enormous feet. Jack was carving a troll, his favorite fairytale creature. When he finished, Jack realized the troll was his best carving ever!

"You are my magical troll!" he declared, wiping the last tears from his face. "All you need now is a magical staff."

Jack picked up a broken twig and glued it to the troll's hand. Then he plucked a purple marble from his toolbox and pasted it on top of the twig. Jack sat down on a pile of hay. He stared at the finished troll.

"Hmm. You need a name. I'm going to call you..." Jack paused. "Zagaboo!"

Jack liked the name because it was really weird and it started with a Z, his favorite letter. No one else in the world would have the name Zagaboo. It was a special name for a very special troll.

Forgetting his troubles, Jack raced out of the barn with Zagaboo. "Mommy! Daddy!" he yelled. "Look at what I made!"

Jack's parents turned and saw Jack running toward them with something in his hand. "We're glad you decided to come back!" Daddy said. "What do you have there?"

"This is Zagaboo! He's my magical troll!" Jack responded, trying to catch his breath.

Jack's parents looked with amazement at the little troll. They loved Zagaboo's big feet, huge nose, and pointy ears.

"You are so talented, Jack," said Mommy. "What kind of magic does Zagaboo do?"

"Zagaboo makes me brave. I can do anything when Zagaboo is with me. Watch!" Jack sat down next to the biggest cow on the farm, placed Zagaboo next to him, and began milking the cow. His parents couldn't believe it. Jack wasn't afraid anymore. Zagaboo really was magic! From that day on, Jack and Zagaboo were best friends. They went everywhere and did everything together. Jack took Zagaboo with him to feed the pigs, to clean up after the horses, and to work on his other chores. Jack also took Zagaboo to school, to play sports, and to go out onto the playground with his friends.

One day, Jack went into town with Daddy. Town was far away and they had to go through the woods to get there. Jack used to be afraid of the woods. He had heard they were filled with tree ghosts and wild animals with special powers. However, Jack wasn't scared that day. He had Zagaboo with him. In fact, Jack was even brave enough to help Daddy steer the horses. In town Jack and Daddy ran many errands. They delivered milk, eggs, and ham to the grocery stores, and picked up feed for the cows as well as firewood to burn in the coming winter.

When they were done, Jack and Daddy climbed into their cart and headed back home. Jack felt great about how much he had helped. But he was so exhausted that he immediately fell asleep.

It was dark in the forest and Daddy didn't see a large rock on the path. As the cart rolled over the rock, Zagaboo bounced out and fell onto the ground. Daddy didn't realize Zagaboo was gone, so he did not stop the cart. Jack was so tired that he did not wake up. The horses kept trotting down the path, leaving Zagaboo far behind.

Zagaboo sat underneath some bushes for several hours until a gopher came by. The gopher was fascinated by the little troll. He thought Zagaboo smelled really good, like walnut. After a few twitches of his nose, the gopher picked up the troll with his teeth and carried him down a nearby hole. He took Zagaboo deep underground through a maze of tunnels and into his favorite chamber directly beneath the tallest tree in the woods.

After circling a few times to find a good spot, the gopher lay Zagaboo down, curled up next to him, and fell asleep. He stayed with the little troll all through winter.

At the start of spring the temperature warmed up, the flowers bloomed, and the birds began to chirp. High above the tunnels, in the branches of the biggest tree in the forest, thousands of special little creatures began waking up. Shelltop Fairies that had nested in the tree throughout winter popped out of their cocoons and stretched their wings.

As it did each spring, magic fairy dust fell from the broken cocoons like snow onto everything below. The dust gave magical powers to all it touched. The roots that absorbed the dust helped the tree grow, which explained why it was so big. The dust made the rabbits jump further, the skunks smell worse, and the gophers dig faster.

Normally, the fairies would talk and play games in the tree after hatching, but that day a big storm had rolled in and the fairies raced into the woods to find shelter.

The rain fell hard and long and washed the fairy dust into large puddles.

The edge of one of the puddles overflowed into a nearby gopher hole and a stream of magic water slowly began weaving its way deep into the underground tunnels, eventually reaching Zagaboo's chamber. The magic water pooled around the little wooden troll and soaked into the fibers of his round little body and huge ears.

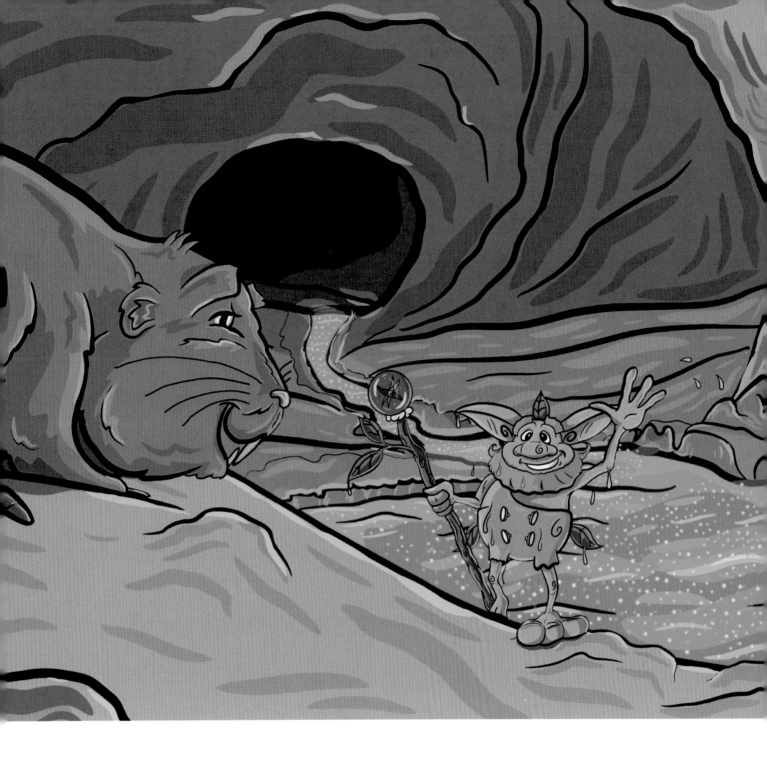

Zagaboo began to glow green. Then he started to move, first with the wiggle of a finger, and then a toe. Before long, his arms and legs began to flop around. Then in one quick motion he sat up, startling the gopher. The little troll paused for a moment, tapped his head a few times to clean the remaining water out of his ears, and then turned toward the gopher. With a big smile he said, "Hello, my furry friend. What might your name be?"

The gopher looked at the troll and twitched his nose with curiosity.

"Alright then," said the troll. "I shall call you Twitch! My name is Zagaboo, and I need to get lots of wood! Will you and the other gophers help me?"

Twitch stomped his feet with excitement and raced off to collect the other gophers. Soon hundreds of gophers returned with enough wood to fill the entire tunnel.

Zagaboo was a great wood carver just like Jack. Picking up a small sharp stone, he dove headfirst into the woodpile, carving troll after troll. He made girl trolls, boy trolls, tall trolls, short trolls, trolls with long hair, trolls with no hair, trolls with big noses, and others with funny hats.

Zagaboo carved thousands of trolls, all of them very different except for their great big ears. When he finished, he dunked each of them into the puddle of magic water to bring them to life. The trolls and gophers gathered around Zagaboo to watch.

After dunking the last troll, Zagaboo raised his staff with the purple marble and announced, "I am Zagaboo, and I am very happy to meet you! Listen to me and I will tell you a story about a boy named Jack."

He told the trolls and gophers how he and Jack were best friends and how he helped Jack become super brave.

"I discovered long ago," said Zagaboo, "that trolls can help children learn how to do anything: how to dance, run, swim, read, fish, play sports, and not be afraid of the woods or the dark, plus many other things. Beneath this mighty tree, we shall build a great magical kingdom filled with fishing ponds, race tracks, dance halls, swimming pools, and enormous jungle gyms. Then we will invite kids from around the world, and they will have the most fun ever as they learn how to become brave and try new things in our kingdom."

The gophers stomped their feet and the trolls cheered with excitement, and they all happily started building Zagaboo's magical kingdom.

Zagaboo patted Twitch on the head and whispered into his ear, "I must go see Jack. Can you take me? I know the way."

Twitch nodded his head and chattered his teeth excitedly. Zagaboo climbed onto Twitch's back and held tightly onto his fur as Twitch raced out of the chamber and through the tunnels.

It wasn't long before they reached a farmhouse with horses, chickens, pigs, and cows, and a big red barn in the back. It was Jack's house! Zagaboo saw Jack's mommy and daddy feeding the horses in the field, but where was Jack? Perhaps he was in his favorite place. Zagaboo asked Twitch to dig a tunnel into the big red barn.

They popped their heads up out of the ground and saw Jack sitting in a pile of hay, carving a piece of wood. Zagaboo quietly climbed out of the tunnel and ran behind a bucket close to Jack. He slowly peeked around the corner.

Jack caught a glimpse of the little troll. Could it be?

"Zagaboo!" Jack yelled "I can't believe it! How did you come alive?"

He raced over to Zagaboo and scooped him up. "I missed you so much," he said, hugging him so tightly that the little troll's ears curled.

Zagaboo could hardly move in Jack's grip, but he finally managed to reach out and tug on Jack's earlobe. Jack began to glow green, and before he knew it, POOF! He had shrunk to the size of a troll! Startled, Jack released Zagaboo and fell backward onto his bottom.

Jack sat on the ground, looking all around. He was amazed by the enormous size of everything. The horses in the stalls were as big as dinosaurs. A dung beetle marching by seemed as large as a dog, and a moth flying above was the size of an eagle. Jack looked at Zagaboo, who was standing above him.

"Let me tell you a secret, Jack." Zagaboo pointed to his ear with his big troll hand. "Magic is in the ears," he said with a big smile.

Jack looked at Zagaboo's great big ears and smiled back.

The troll sat down on a mound of dirt. He told Jack how he had fallen off the back of his daddy's cart while Jack was asleep, and about the magic water, and how he lived in a kingdom with trolls and gophers in the woods underneath the biggest tree in the forest. He also told Jack about the fairies living in the trees, and how all the animals there had magical powers.

'Those must be the tree ghosts and wild animals I used to be afraid of in the forest,' Jack thought. This was the best story ever!

Zagaboo then asked Jack if he was still being brave and trying new things.

"When I woke up," Jack told him, "and you weren't in the cart, I got so worried that I would be afraid of everything again. I told Daddy I wanted to go back into the woods and look for you. We went back the next day and searched all over the forest, but we couldn't find you. When the sun started going down, I realized I had spent all day in the woods without you, and I wasn't even scared. Right then I knew that I could do anything all by myself! When I went back home, I learned how to swim in the river and I climbed the biggest tree on the farm. And every day I would milk the cows and feed the chickens, pigs, and horses."

"That's great, Jack! I was hoping you'd say that!" said Zagaboo.

Then Zagaboo lifted up his staff, which began to glow purple, and touched Jack on the shoulder. Jack started to glow purple as well.

"I hereby dub you Jack the brave, graduate of the Kingdom of Zagaboo!"

Jack stuck out his chest and smiled. He was so proud!

"Well, Jack," said Zagaboo, "It sounds like you don't need my help anymore. However, there are many other kids in the world who still need to find their bravery to try new things. My kingdom of trolls and I want to help them become brave and adventurous like you. Please tell your friends about me and my kingdom!"

Jack nodded his head in agreement.

"Before your friends go to bed," Zagaboo explained, "they must pinch one ear and say, 'Zagaboo, Zagaboo, where are you?' If they do this, the marble on my staff will glow purple and I will know they need me. Once they fall asleep and begin to dream, I will send special trolls to invite them back to my magical kingdom, where they will have great adventures and learn many amazing things. Can you do that Jack? Can you tell your friends?"

"Yes, I will tell them Zagaboo," Jack said with excitement.

"Thank you, Jack," said Zagaboo. "I'm very proud of you. I can see that you're brave enough to do anything now. But if you ever need me again, just pinch your ear and say, 'Zagaboo, Zagaboo, where are you?' and I'll come find you right away."

Jack gave Zagaboo another great big hug. "I'll never forget you, Zagaboo."

Zagaboo reached out and tugged on the boy's ear. Jack began to glow green, and slowly grew back to normal size. Jack gazed down at Zagaboo and Twitch. Zagaboo waved at Jack and yelled, "The magic is in the ears, Jack! Never forget that!"

Zagaboo climbed onto Twitch's back and held on tightly. The gopher stomped his feet a few times, and they both raced back into the tunnels toward Zagaboo's kingdom.

The next day Jack told all his friends about Zagaboo. His friends told their friends, and they in turn told others. Eventually, everyone in the whole world knew about the little troll and his kingdom.

And that's how the legend of Zagaboo was born.

Some people say Zagaboo isn't real. Perhaps he isn't. Nobody can prove it either way. But one night, before you go to sleep, try pulling on your ear and saying, "Zagaboo, Zagaboo, where are you?" Maybe, just maybe, you'll find out he is real. If you do, be sure to tell your mommy and daddy about your amazing adventures and what you learned in Zagaboo's kingdom!

The End

Made in the USA
Lexington, KY
23 July 2018